I0691031

Get Out of My Dream!

William A. Glasser

Published by Open Books

Copyright © 2019 by William A. Glasser

All rights reserved. No part of this book may be reproduced, scanned, or distributed in any printed or electronic form without permission except in the case of brief quotations embodied in critical articles and reviews.

Interior design by Siva Ram Maganti

Cover image "Paper art of Goodnight and sweet dream, night and origami mobile concept, vector art and illustration" © Vezunchik shutterstock.com/g/Chernyshov+Alexander

ISBN-13: 978-1948598217

—◦⚘◦—

Chapter 1

ALL RIGHT, SO I have a good imagination. But how would you feel if you woke up one morning and you saw what I am looking at now. The dresser out a bit from the wall, the small picture hanging above it, the kitchen chair beside my bed, even the clothes I had tossed across it. They are all glowing softly at me with a strange light that has to be coming from somewhere other than this world.

Yes, I know, it's quite a leap. But as I look more closely at the light, it isn't just glowing at me. It's blinking away in what appears to be some kind of a crazy, mixed-up pattern. And it keeps repeating that same pattern, until it really startles me as I suddenly recognize what it is. I sit up in bed now, staring at the light, having a hard time believing it, for apparently someone is sending me a bit of Morse code. Three blinks, then two blinks, then three more. It's a plea for help. An SOS. But where can it be coming from? And how can I possibly respond to it?

I keep looking at the light until it suddenly begins to trouble me, for it is beginning now to make me feel rather tired. I lie down again, trying to stop the feeling, but my eyes just seem to be closing by themselves, slowly shutting out all the things I see around me in my room. Fortunately, though, it lasts for only a few moments. And then, with a big sigh of relief, I find that I can open my eyes again. Well, at least I think I have opened them, until I look at what is around me now.

What is this place? Where have I gone?

Apparently, I'm still asleep, and I must be dreaming now. Is that it? It must be a dream. Including that guy who is standing in the shadows over there, staring at me with a most unpleasant look.

Chapter 2

Okay, then, so I'm still asleep, though it's certainly not one of my own better dreams that I find myself in now. Usually, I meet more interesting people than the only other guy I can see. Well, I should have expected it. Another one of my many disappointments, along with the heaviest one I'm already carrying around.

In college I had majored in literature, spending a few wonderful years reading the world's greatest works, until I finally had completed my degree. It was a world changing experience for me, to meet so many perceptive minds. They had not only opened my eyes to what was often hidden beneath the surface of everything I saw around me. Through their carefully crafted works of literature, they had also taken me out to the very edges of this world, and at times even beyond those edges, to new worlds they had created so brilliantly that I would often find myself existing within them. Standing in the bow of a whale ship, with a harpoon gripped in my hand, as the boat heads into the edge of the foam being raised by a whale's thrashing tale. Or with my lance raised high, as I ride on Rosinante, going forth to do battle with the giant windmills.

And so, having recently earned my degree, I headed out into the world of work, with a confident smile, and high expectations, to discover that nobody I talked with seemed to be at all interested in why Dante's Comedy was so Divine, or what Alice was doing in Wonderland, or anything else I had read. I had also mailed out three applications for the job I thought would be really great. An editor in a publishing company. But I didn't get a single response.

So here I am now, with no job yet, and not a penny left in my pocket, stuck every day in this little room I have rented above a garage, where I can't even have a decent dream to get my head out of here.

Well, then, how about an indecent one? Or any other kind of dream that's at least a bit more interesting than this drab-looking one I find myself standing in now. It appears to be a country setting, but there is only one sad-looking tree in sight, just off there a bit to the right, along with a hodge-podge of scraggly bushes strewn around the entire area. And that's just not the way it should be. I mean, if `I have to be dreaming now, then I'd rather imagine something much more entertaining than this, like having a pleasant lunch, say, at a grand hotel with William Shakespeare or Herman Melville. Or even just an afternoon tea with someone like Edgar Allan

Poe, who could likely come up with a way for me to get rid of that man standing over there, who is really beginning to irritate me. Like an old stone statue, a gray one lurking in the shadows underneath that tree, he hasn't moved at all, except for that nasty look he keeps giving me. And it seems that he's twisting his face into an even tighter scowl, as his eyes begin to burn with an intensity that will not let me look away any more.

Suddenly, I catch a glimpse of something out of the corner of my eye. It's streaking down toward me from high up in that tree nearby, trailing a glowing light behind it, a light that makes me think of—Wham! It strikes the side of my head now, knocking me softly onto the ground. Softly? I thought it was going to knock my head off. But then it lands beside me, and I can finally see what it is.

Or, more likely, what it is not, for I have never seen any creature like it. Not even in a dream. Animal or vegetable? I'm really not sure. It's simply a large ball, maybe twice as big as my head, with long hairs spiking out from it in all directions, completely covering over whatever might be there inside them. I can't see anything else that is sticking out from it, like some kind of an arm or a leg maybe. So how is it able to move, then? And how does it communicate? It looks like I won't be having any kind of meaningful contact with it.

But suddenly it takes me by surprise, as some hairs on the side that is facing me begin moving apart.

And within the spot that is cleared now, I can see two glistening eyes that are staring right back at me. Apparently, I am the one who is now being watched. And, I assume, being checked out.

Then another surprise, as a soft, glowing light from deep within those glistening eyes radiates out to me, and begins pulsing in that pattern I saw back in my room.

"Hey," I say, "was that you? Did you send me that message I got?"

I wait a moment, expecting no reply, until it suddenly blares out, "ESS OH ESS!" And then a very tiny voice says, "Hear me now? Here I am."

"But where?" I say. "I can hardly see you, underneath all of those hairs."

"Hairs are good," it slowly says, "whenever a Gloom is looking my way."

"But I still don't know what you are," I say. "Do you have a name? What should I call you?"

The little voice begins to twitter, like it might be laughing now. "Well, I'm a Gleamer. A happy one. And I always did want a name of my own. So what would you like to call me?"

"All right," I say, pausing a moment, as I remember how gently it had hit me in the head. I reach out now and brush my hand across the very ends of its hairs. They are not at all spikes. They are pleasantly soft. And a few of them curl around the tips of my fingers, like maybe it's shaking hands with me. Whatever it's doing, thankfully, it does not appear to be at all aggressive. So I smile, as it comes to me. "I think I'd like to call you Softy."

The twittering comes even louder now. "Yes! Yes! I like that name!"

"A lot better than Gloom," I say. "But who is he? And why is he called that?"

"He is the one who keeps watching you," Softy says. "So you must be extra careful, for he knows now that you are here."

I glance over and see that the man is still there, staring at me from the shadows of that sad looking tree, and those burning eyes appear to be opening wider now.

"No! No!" Softy cries. "Stop doing that!"

"Stop doing what?" I say, as I turn away. "I was just looking. Is that a problem?"

"You haven't told me your name yet," Softy says.

"My name is Lester," I say. "Please call me Les."

"Well, Les," he says, "if you had kept looking at him, as he was looking directly at you, he would have turned your light completely off. And you must never let that happen."

"Turned off what light? I don't understand."

"The light within you. The source of your life." Softy is getting intense now, imploring me to understand.

"So he's some kind of bad guy? Is that it?"

"The very worst," Softy says. "He's a scouting party, for all the other Glooms. Up to this point, we have always managed to keep our distance from them. We have stayed in our own territory, and the Glooms have stayed in theirs. But here he is now, the first Gloom to come this far into Gleamer territory."

"But why is he here?" I say. "What does he want?"

"Well, that's what's troubling me," Softy says. "They seem to be up to something new. Something involving our main defense." He looks down at the Gloom again. "But I don't know what it is yet. And I'm hoping it's not what I have in mind."

"So you do have one, then," I say. "I mean, a way to defend yourselves."

"Yes, we have," Softy says. "What has kept them within their own territory is their fear of the force that we can achieve when all of our lights are brought together into a single devastating beam."

"But what about your visitor, then? Is he somehow different from all the others?" I glance down at him, but it doesn't help. "He stays in the shadows under that tree, so I can't see what he really looks like."

"Well," Softy says, "they're hard to describe. But perhaps I can pick out a few of your words from that amazing collection you are carrying around." And he turns now to look at me, apparently wanting to see my reaction "A Gloom looks like an unwrapped mummy, walking in Frankenstein's shoes of lead."

I almost break out laughing at that. It sounds more like a punchline to someone's silly joke. But I do manage to hold it in, for it's obviously not at all funny to Softy, as he explains to me why now.

"That Gloom, I believe, is looking for some way to avoid the full force of our protective beam." Just saying it appears to be troubling him deeply. "If he ever did find a way, Les, he would then signal it back to the others, and they would soon be arriving here, every single one of them, to stop us from creating another deadly beam."

"And what would happen then, Softy? I still don't understand."

"If they managed to turn off the light within us?" His large round eyes, which were focused on me now, seemed to dim for a moment at the thought. "It would make us all, forever after, disappear into darkness."

Chapter 3

Softy appears to be studying me now, looking for I don't know what, until he finally nods, as though he has found it. "And that is why we are pleading with you to Save Our Souls. We are desperate, and we need your help, for you are the only one we know who can find the way to stop them."

Softy is the only Gleamer I've seen here. So where are all the other ones? Or are they already hiding now?

I keep standing here, trying for something better than the feeble excuse I now offer him. "Of course I'd be glad to help, Softy. But you would first have to tell me how."

The heavy quivers are suddenly back, as Softy announces in a loud voice, "He's going to help! He says he will do it!"

From behind every scraggly bush around us, as far off as I can see, a Gleamer suddenly steps into view, and they all quickly gather together into a large crowd that begins moving toward us, keeping their distance away from the tree where the Gloom is still standing. And as they get nearer to us, they begin filling the air with their twittering now, like a hearty round of applause for me.

"Oh, Softy," I say. "Didn't you hear me? I have no idea of what should be done, or even who I can turn to for help." And that really confuses me. Pick and choose who I'm going to talk to? I mean, can that be done in a dream? I don't believe it.

"Of course you do!" Softy says. "And of course you can!" He sounds like he's laughing. "How very delightful you are, Les! What you really have no idea of is just how special you actually are, for you are filled to overflowing with it, giving you everything you will need. And that is why we have singled you out."

I pause for a moment, but I'm still lost. "Filled with what? A lot of hot air? You have to stop confusing me, Softy."

"Filled," he says, and his eyes are now glowing, "with the many wonderful people you have gathered within you, for they have not only enriched your life, Les. They have also brightened your light for you. So if you want to turn to someone for help, you just have to look inside yourself."

"Wonderful people, inside of me?" Smiling, I shake my head. "How about one or two examples? That might clear things up a bit."

"How about more than two?" he says. "Like Sherlock Holmes, the great detective. And Lancelot, the castle defender. And, obviously, Buffy the Vampire

Slayer, who would be more than happy to meet the Glooms. And Henry Fleming, whose bravery in battle earns him the red badge of courage. And—"

"Enough!" I shout. "These are not real people. And how do you even know about them? Not from me. I've never told you." And then it suddenly dawns on me. "Oh, Softy, please don't tell me. Those eyes of yours, those radiant eyes. Have you been reading what's in my mind?"

His eyes, apparently, can also smile. "Only the residual materials that are still in there. Nothing that you are thinking now."

"Weirder and weirder." I have to stop shaking my head so much. "But like I said, they are not real people."

"And what do you mean by that?" he says.

"I mean that each of them is not an actual living person, but just a product of some author's mind. A figment of his imagination." Wait a minute, I tell myself, as I remember how easy it was for me to lose sight of my own world as I read my way into theirs. "Well, I do have to admit, Softy, that they are, indeed, remarkable characters, for they have often made me cross the line that separates my world from theirs, even leaving me at times wondering which is the real one."

"Like now, you mean?" Softy says.

He's obviously caught me off base. "Well, not really," I say, and I try to make it back to first. "It's more like the first time I saw an elephant. I mean, when I was just a little kid. I couldn't believe that it was real, until the zookeeper let me touch it. And when you whacked me in the head, Softy, I didn't have to struggle with whether you were there or not, for things in a dream just never seem to get that solid."

"Never *seem*?" he says, stressing the word. And if he had eyebrows, he would surely have raised them, for he was clearly enjoying himself.

"All right," I say, wanting to change the subject. "But shouldn't you be keeping your mind on all those Glooms you told me about?"

"Fair enough," he says, "if we both do it. So can you tell me the answer to the question now? How are you going to stop them from coming?"

"A good question," I say, "but I don't have an answer. I mean, I just don't know enough yet. And neither, apparently, do the Glooms. You called him a scouting party, Softy, so he must be here to gather information, the kind that they will all want when they finally do arrive."

"What kind would that be?" Softy says.

"Like how many Gleamers they're going to find here." And then it strikes me, how little I know.

"Thirty-two," he says. "We're a small group."

"And what about the Glooms?" I watch him, as he pauses a moment. "Do you have any idea, Softy? It would be good to know."

His hairs give a little flip. "I'm not sure how to answer, Les. They have always stayed in their territory, as we have always done in ours. Until, that is, this recent visitor caused us to make a quick check on them, and it looked like they were all getting ready to pay us a visit. So judging just from what we saw, I'd say there would probably be about as many of them as us."

"And, unfortunately," I say, "you are all so much smaller."

"And, fortunately," he says, "we are all so much faster. Wait until you see one of them walking. Like I told you, Les, you'd see Frankenstein again, dragging along those lead shoes."

"However slow they might be, Softy, what if they just decide to surround you?" I'm groping for any possibility. "If you found yourselves, say, all crowded together into a much smaller space, how long would you be able to survive, then? And what if they also cut your food supply off?"

"That," says Softy, sounding more cheerful, "would be no problem at all for us. We would just have to open our hairs to enjoy a wide variety of what nourishes us. Like the sunlight, of course, with its strong flavor, and the more subtle moonlight we find so tasty, along with a gentle sprinkling of stars that you might call a dash of herbs, Les."

I have to smile. "It sounds like you're ordering dinner in one of our best restaurants. And that leaves me hoping for a good dessert. How far is their territory from where we are standing now?"

"Oh," Softy says, "a considerable distance. For you, I mean, since you would have to walk there."

"Okay," I say, "then back to our problem." I surprise

myself a bit, for I'm starting to enjoy the dream. "What do you think should be done next?"

"We have all been hoping," Softy says, "that you would be the one to tell us. Do you have any possible answers yet?"

"Yes," I say. "I think I do. Or at least I know where I can find one."

"And that is … ?" Softy says.

"On such a pleasant day," I say, "I think we should take a nice stroll."

He watches me for a moment to see if I'm serious. "And how will that help us with the Glooms?"

"Because," I say, "that's where we will stroll. Let's walk on up there and see for ourselves."

"To Gloomland?" Softy says, and I can hear the tension in his voice. "A pleasant stroll into an area that has never been touched by sunlight? And, to stop us from ever returning again, how about the many traps they have now hidden along the way in the darkest shadows?"

He lets me take it all in, and then he caps it off. "I'm doing my best here, Les, to help you understand how dangerous it will be for us to go so near to them again."

"Not as dangerous," I say, "as just doing nothing, and waiting for them to come here. We need our own scouting party now, if we're going to discover something among them that might show us how to stop them." All right, so I'm getting caught up in it. But why not? It's just what I wanted. Finally, something different. And really, in its own way, kind of entertaining, too.

Softy then turns and raises his voice as he announces to all the others before us, who haven't stopped twittering yet with excitement.

"His next step," he says loudly, above all the twittering, "is to take a stroll to Gloomland! He wants to see it for himself!"

Suddenly, there's not a sound, and not a single movement among them. All I can see are thirty-one pairs of unblinking, disbelieving eyes.

‑◦ ❧ ◦‑

Chapter 4

"JUST THE TWO OF US?" I say.

"Yes," Softy says. "I can show you the way, without putting anyone else in danger."

We are still on the slope, looking down at all the others who had come out earlier from behind all those scraggly bushes.

He raises his voice again. "Stay alert, please, all of you! And return to our territory, where we will hopefully bring you back good news!"

When we begin to make our way down the slope, they start twittering loudly once again, as though sending us off with another cheer. I follow Softy closely as he heads off to the left of the group. Apparently he wants to stay clear of the tree, where the Gloom is still watching everything that is happening around him.

Hurrying along as well as I can, I'm already having trouble keeping up. "Softy," I say, trying to slow him down, "did you ever try to peek a bit into the Gloom's mind? It could certainly give us a lot of information."

"Indeed, it could," Softy says. "But, unfortunately, it would just be a waste of time."

"Sounds like you already tried it," I say. "What was it that you found there?"

"Just what I thought I'd find," he says. "Not a single ray of light in there, Les. It's too dark to see anything."

"What, then, does that tell us?" I say. "I mean, as you so well described, you need the light not only to see, but also to nourish yourself. So what do they feed on?"

He's about to tell me, when I interrupt him. "Wait a minute! I bet I know! Kind of obvious, isn't it. If the Gleamers nourish themselves on light, then the Glooms must surely be feeding on darkness. A wide variety of their own, I bet. Beginning, say, with a tasty salad of the leaf-shadows they gather from beneath evening trees. And then, of course, the main entrée, a pungent serving of total darkness, underneath an overcast sky. To be followed with a special dessert, a slice, no doubt, of blackberry pie. And then the perfect way for them to announce the end of that delicious meal. A low and very dark burp."

"Obviously," Softy says, "we eat in different restaurants. If that was the only difference we had, we could probably get along with them."

"But you also mean them no harm," I say. "They have to be aware of that. So why are they turning against you, Softy? What is making them want to destroy you now?"

"Something," he says, "must have changed among them, since the last time we checked on them. But I have no idea what it might be."

"Sounds like we need a scouting mission, Softy." I'm trying not to smile.

"All right," he says. "One point for you, Les. So let's go and have a look, and see if anything is different there."

"I assume we're on the right path," I say. "Anything else that I should know?"

"Nothing at the moment," he says. "Just follow that yellow brick road ahead, and keep an eye out for flying monkeys."

Well, it isn't exactly yellow. More like the color of dirt. But it is at least a road, and it does help me to walk a bit faster. Including, apparently, Softy, too, who once again starts leaving me struggling behind to stay up with him.

It proves to be quite a challenge for me, as Softy holds to his fast pace. But then I find that I'm now doing rather well at keeping up with him, and it's making me feel pretty pleased with myself.

Until, that is, I begin to see what is really cheering me up, for it's not just my keeping up with Softy. As I glance around at the countryside that the road is taking us through, I am caught by how bright and alive everything around me is looking. The trees, the bushes, the fields of grass. With the sunlight shining down upon them, they are all so vibrantly full of life that they seem to be inviting me to share with them the wonderful feeling of how intensely green they are.

I glance at Softy, and I have to frown, for he doesn't seem to be looking off at either side. "Don't you see it, Softy? Can't you feel it at all? We're surrounded by such a welcoming sight. I'm beginning to think that maybe our stroll is going to be a very pleasant one."

Softy just keeps moving ahead, as though he can't look away from the road. "A pleasant feeling, indeed, Les, especially if you prove to be right. But I'm not quite ready to join you there, for what I am feeling, and much stronger, is the need to keep an eye out for both of us."

"Maybe," I say, "we should change your name, then. How about from Softy to Grumpy?"

"One of the seven dwarfs?" he says.

"Yes," I say. "I think it fits you, the way I hear you talking."

"Well, it's better than Dopey," he says. "Then I would have to keep listening to you, and do whatever you might want."

"Nothing wrong with that," I say. "Is there any reason why you shouldn't?"

"Many more than one," he says. "Like what we're walking into. Your turn to look, Les. Anything new?"

As we keep walking, I keep looking, trying to find whatever might be troubling Softy. And the first thing I notice is that everything out there, as far as I can see, is no longer glistening green with reflected sunlight. "Okay," I say. "It's the light, isn't it. It all seems to be dimming down. So what does that mean, Softy?"

"It means," he says, "that we have finally arrived at our destination, the outer boundary of Gloomland." And he looks around, in every direction, wanting to be sure that they are not nearby.

"Okay," I say. "So what happens if we just keep walking into it? Does everything slowly get darker and darker?"

"Well, we'll just have to see." And he looks around, checking again. "But remember what we're here for, Les. It's a two-sided scouting we're on. They want to destroy us completely. But they haven't been able to do it yet. So we need to be sure that nothing here has been changed into a new threat. We, in turn, want to destroy them, and we also don't know how. But if they ever did make a move against us, there is one thing we do know. We don't want to just stop them, Les, and then start waiting for the next threat. This time, once and for all, we need to defeat them completely. Which brings us back to why we're here, looking also for a way to do it."

"Quite an interesting race," I say. "Winner apparently takes all."

"And the losers?" He waits to hear my answer.

But I don't really have one, so I just shrug. "Not a problem at all, Softy. There won't be any losers left."

And so we set off once more, at a much slower pace, as we both begin searching for anything different that we might see in Gloomland. But I have to ask myself. Different from what? It's my first time here, so how would I know what might have changed? I'm about to raise that point with Softy, but he seems so caught up in his own search that I decide to drop it and just go along, looking for anything that could be troubling.

Like that tiny, odd-looking plant over there. The one, I mean, that looks as if it's upside-down, with its roots raised straight up into the air, and the top of it growing down into the ground. I puzzle over it for a while, until I finally give in.

"Softy," I say, "it's your fault."

"What do you mean, Les?" He has paused to look at me.

"You said we should keep an eye out for anything different. Something that might prove to be a threat. Like that little plant. The one over there." I point to show him, hoping to amuse him, and to keep things on the light side, since we're heading toward what should be the darkest center of Gloomland.

Softy goes over to the plant, and he stays there a while, as though he's studying it. "Another interesting example, Les. A particularly well chosen one."

"Of what?" I say. "I thought it was funny."

"Of how things here have adapted," he says, "to the Glooms moving into their area. Remember what they always do to any life form filled with light."

I look again at the little plant. "Are you saying that what it's doing there is kind of hiding its head, Softy?"

"Exactly," he says. "Like you might also be doing very shortly, if we cannot find a way to stop them."

I try not to shake the head that I may have to hide

soon. "Isn't there any outer limit to all the weirdness in this place?"

"Of course there is," Softy says. "We just crossed it a short while ago. Welcome again to Gloomland."

Chapter 5

ONCE AGAIN, WE BOTH start walking, and we keep at it for quite a while, until I actually start to get a little bored. Except for that odd little plant I saw, the countryside we are walking through doesn't seem to be all that different from what we had walked through to get here. But we keep at it, with no complaints, until a breeze that is coming toward us softly begins to blow away some of the bright sunlight around us, dimming our sight of the road and the trees.

"What now?" I ask Softy. "Time for a nap?"

"No sleeping on the job," he says, quivering a soft laugh. "Maybe we still have some time left, so let's see how long the light lasts." And he starts off again into another one of his challenging paces.

I try to keep up, as well as I can, and since it doesn't seem to be getting any darker, we both go back to checking out whatever we are able to see, on both sides of the road. And that, at least, confirms for me that we are still heading toward our ultimate goal, for the setting around us is slowly becoming so dismal and depressing that we must be getting further into the deepest parts of this aptly named place.

Except, maybe, for the trees. The big ones, I mean, with the branches reaching out all the way across the road. I'm relieved to see that some rays of sunlight are still making their way down through the branches, lighting up the road a bit just below them. And also lighting up the palm of my hand, which I am pleased to openly offer them as I pass under each of the trees. Smiling now, I quickly close my fist on a handful of the glistening rays, like maybe I'll carry them along with me, to cheer me up while I keep searching. But, on second thought, I change my mind, for this place clearly needs them more than I do. And when I open my palm again, like I'm letting free a few butterflies, I stand there, frozen for a moment, unable to look away, for what I am holding now is a handful of darkness.

"Softy!" I almost scream his name, as I keep staring at my hand.

Before I can call out again, I look down, and he's there beside me.

"What is it, Les?" He is staring at me.

"This," I say. And I hold out my hand.

When he looks at it, he starts away. "Quickly. Just ahead on the road."

And as fast as I can, I stumble after him, trying not to let my hand touch any other part of me, until we come to a place where the sun is still lighting up a fairly large section of the road.

"Hold out your hand," Softy cries. "And turn it up to the sun. And stay that way, until I tell you that you can move again."

I do what he says, but without looking to see if it is still there, for I can feel the fear that is gripping me, as I picture it spreading up my arm, and then throughout the rest of me, leaving me as lifeless as … what? Another Gloom?

"What's happening here?" I say. "What did I do?"

"You squeezed out more than just the sunbeams, Les, leaving your palm without any light." He comes closer to check out my hand. "You have to keep in mind where we are. Gloomland has its own peculiar ways, and most of them are not very pleasant. Unless, of course, you're already a Gloom. But I don't think you're there yet."

"All right," I say. "I'll keep it in mind. But if we're just at the very edge of Gloomland, and it's already shaking hands with me, how much further into it before I become a voting member?"

"That depends," he says, "on whether we want to continue our scouting mission. We have not discovered anything yet that might stop them if they come our way. But I will leave it up to you, Les. You did have quite a scare."

I take in a deep breath, risking it since we're still in the sunlight, and I slowly let it out, as I try to relax. "All right, let's give it another try, as long as we can still see where we're going."

But as we set off again, going deeper into Gloom-land, the sunlight ahead of me shining on the road, and beneath each of the trees we pass, seems to be retreating, leaving behind a dimness that is making it harder for me to see much more than a short way up the road ahead, and just a few of the shrubs and trees right along the edge of it.

"Keep a sharp eye out," Softy says, "for anything different you might see."

"No problem," I say. "An easy task, since there's so little that I can see." But maybe, I think, some music might help. Something fitting for the mood I'm in. Like a chorus singing a funeral dirge.

Suddenly, without any warning, as most things seem to happen here, Softy jolts me to a quick stop. "Don't move," he says. "Don't even blink. Sometimes they can't see us, then."

We both stand there, frozen in place, until Softy finally turns to me, and with the flip of a few hairs, gestures to something ahead.

Just off to the right, in the near darkness, somebody is sitting underneath that small tree beside the road.

"Softy," I say, "is that what I think, or am I losing it?"

"Careful, Les," Softy says.

But I can't resist taking a couple of steps so that I can see him better, for this will be my first, and maybe my last, close-up look at a Gloom.

As I get nearer to him, he doesn't move at all. He just keeps sitting there, in the darkness, and I can't see his face. So I'm wondering, is he also watching me?

Softy chimes in again, taking no chances. "Whatever else you might do, Les, don't look directly into his eyes."

"Don't worry," I say. "It's much too dark here for me even to see them."

I'm beginning to feel a bit frustrated, for I can hardly see anything at all, and I don't want to miss this opportunity. If I only had a flashlight. Or even just a candle, maybe. Or—wait a minute! I jam my left hand into the pocket of my pants, remembering what is there. A small cigarette lighter! I'm not a smoker, but I do occasionally burn off some of my rubbish in the grill outside. With that in mind, I usually keep it there in my pocket. And though it doesn't make very much of a flame, it's better than nothing. So I click it on.

The flame is indeed small, casting very little light as I hold it up before him. But what it lets me see is an awkwardly molded lump of clay, shaped into a gray and lifeless face, with only one eye open. The other one stays closed. When the Gloom suddenly begins to move, raising his hand up, I get ready to make a quick retreat. But all he does with his hand, and very slowly, is to reach out toward the little flame, until one of his fingers touches it. With a heavy grunt, and a quick jerk, he pulls his hand back again. Then he holds it up in front of his face, looking at his fingertip, until he lowers it again, and he looks at me.

His one eye, with a strong look that I can't quite figure out, is staring intently at me. But I don't get any sense of a threat coming from it.

Remembering Softy's warning, however, I quickly turn away. "What should we do with him, Softy? I mean, we don't need a pet, so let's not take him home with us."

Softy is also closely studying the Gloom. "I wonder what he has inside him, Les. That could be a useful piece of information."

I glance back once again at the Gloom. "Like maybe does he bleed, Softy? A very tempting thought, indeed. Why don't I give him a poke, say, with a sharply pointed stick?"

As Softy turns to look at me, I add, "Only kidding."

"Glad to hear that, Les," Softy says. "But it still leaves me at a loss. Perhaps he has badly hurt himself. Or he could be sick with something they catch."

"Or," I add, "he just might be taking a break, after setting up one of those traps you mentioned. With that in mind, I think I'll vote for the sharply pointed stick."

Before Softy could respond, we have to back up quickly, for the Gloom suddenly starts to get up. And when he does, he just stands there, still looking at me with that one eye. Wanting to put some distance between us, I'm about to take off, with a warning shout to Softy, when the Gloom finally turns around, and we watch him lumbering off into the scattering of bushes and trees that close behind him, until he is out of sight.

"A very interesting meeting, indeed," I say, for, as the Gloom had slowly walked away, what came to mind was an old saying I had always liked: In the land of the blind, the one-eyed man is king.

"Don't get too carried away," Softy says. "What you may have just seen is a Gloom with a problem A very serious problem, indeed."

"I don't understand," I say. "What kind of a problem would a Gloom have?"

"The Glooms are not at all kind," he says, "to any one of them with a physical difference. Apparently, because he has only one eye, I would not be surprised to hear that they had banished him from Gloomland. And that may be why we found him there, sitting alone beside the road. Until, thank goodness, he stood up, and headed off away from us."

His voice can't hide the relief he is feeling. "Tell me, though, what did you do to make that little light on his face?"

"It was my lighter," I say. "I didn't remember that I had it with me."

"What's a lighter?" he says.

"It makes a flame," I say, "when you want to light something."

"Interesting," he says. "But what's a flame?"

"A flame is just a bit of fire." I shrug, like it's kind of obvious.

"Okay," he says. "Now what is fire?"

I look at him. Is he kidding me? But he keeps looking right back, clearly waiting for my answer. So apparently the Gloom is not the only one who has never seen fire.

"All right, Softy," I say. "Maybe this will tell you. Just poke one of your hairs very quickly into it, and that should let you know what it is. But quickly, Softy. I don't want to hurt you."

When I click the lighter and hold it out to him, Softy lifts up one of his hairs, and he jabs it in and out of the flame.

"Ouch!" he says. "It did hurt. But why, Les? I don't understand."

"Hard to explain," I say. "But it could be like what a Gloom feels when you shine your light at him, only a lot stronger than that, for what really hurts is the heat in the flame. It's very intense, and you have to be careful, because it could seriously damage you. Like ending your existence, Softy. Would that be strong enough for you?"

"All right," he says. "So let's make a deal. If you don't look directly into any Gloom's eyes, I'll not stick any part of me directly into a flame."

"Fair enough," I say.

"Then let's keep going," he says. "At least for a bit longer. It could be a good sign that we haven't yet discovered anything troubling here." And as he sets off down the road again, with a more uplifting pace this time, I do my best to keep up with him. But we haven't gone very far at all until I have to admit that I won't be able to last much longer, and I start thinking about falling back and just taking it easy for a while.

Until, that is, Softy suddenly puts on the brakes again, and I skid to a halt right next to him.

31

"Perhaps," he says, "I've spoken too soon, for I don't like the looks of that, Les."

Ahead of us, just off to the right, an unusually large tree is growing, with its branches reaching out almost across the entire road. And the shadow it is casting down onto the road, mixing in with the sunlight there, looks like a large spider web.

"A bit too creepy for me," I say. "Do you think it's one of those traps you mentioned?"

"It could well be," he said. "We've been making such good progress, they may be trying to scare us off from going any further."

"Well," I say, "if that's what they're up to, they're not doing a very good job of it. Just look at all the sunlight, Softy. It's back to lighting the way for us. Including on the road there, right under the tree that's troubling you. But if it's still bothering you, then one of us will have to show the other one how brave he is."

Softy twitters, as though he's chuckling. "Let's try neither of us, then, so we won't be arguing about who is going to gain all the glory." And he moves to the other side of the road, where his hairs reach out and curl around a small stick that is lying on the ground. Then he returns again, and, as he stands beside me, he flips the stick ahead, and it lands beneath the tree.

Quickly, we have to back away, for out of the tree a large net suddenly drops onto the road, where we could easily have been standing.

"A net?" I say, not very impressed. "Is that the best that they can do?"

"Oh, Les," he says, "It's just the beginning."

Before he can say anything more, holy hell breaks loose, for what the net has apparently caught is the sunlight still shining on the road, just underneath the tree. And I watch, amazed, as the net keeps closing its grip more tightly around the beams, as though it is squeezing the life from them, while they twist and struggle to break free of the grip, until all that remains for me to see, as the net rises back up out of sight, is the dark shadow left behind on the road just under the tree.

"And that," says Softy, "could have been us, with every glimmer of our light squeezed completely out of us. It also tells us why they have decided to confront us."

I'm staring at him, as he turns to me, for I'm still too caught up in what had just happened. "What was it, Softy? What have they done?"

"We can call it an LD," he says. "It's a Light Destructor. Their first one. We knew that something like this might well be possible to make, Les, but we always thought that such an advanced concept would be far beyond their limited abilities to achieve it. And yet clearly they have just proven us wrong. Which means that their next step will likely be a mobile one that they can take wherever they want."

"A mobile one?" I say, trying to imagine it. "What would they do with it, if they could build it?"

"Oh," he says, "it's a Gloomer's dream. They could never stand the light, Les, that we have always used to keep them away. But that, I'm afraid, has completely changed, so they will surely be coming soon. And if we just wait for them to arrive, I have no doubt about what that will lead to. A total and terribly destructive war, with a complete devastation of our territory." He turns and looks directly at me. "Do you understand what that means. Les? The only choice we are left with now? Before they ever reach our borders, we absolutely have to stop them. And I do mean we, Les, especially you. So whatever you can come up with to stop them, it will have to be something entirely new, not only to us, but also to them."

I hear his plea, loud and clear, and he pauses a moment to let me respond. But I just keep standing there, with my mind still caught up in what I had seen in that net.

"All right," he says. "One more time. Can you tell me what it might be, Les? Do you have any idea at all?"

Something entirely new, not only to Softy, but also to the Glooms? I want to reply so badly that I can feel the ache throbbing away inside me. But when nothing comes to me, I have to tell him. "No, Softy. I really don't. It has all become so complicated that I can't even think any more. Except about the Glooms, and what they will do when they get there."

"Then let us hope," Softy says, "that time will be on our side, for we will have to go now to the mountain, and seek the guidance of Brian."

"Sitting up on a mountain, is he?" I have to smile. "So Brian must be one of your wise ones?"

"Yes," Softy says, "a wise one, indeed, for Brian

means a double brain. Let me spell it out for you, Les." And he looks at me with innocent eyes.

"Come on," I say, with a bigger smile. "Maybe, instead of Brian, we should go and see his dog, for if we flip the d and g around, we'll be talking with an even higher up guy. Do you want me to spell it out for you?"

"I'm serious, Les," Softy says. And, with a twinge of regret, I can see that he really is.

"Well," I say, "you'll have to excuse me. But why do we just keep wandering deeper and deeper into all the weirdness here?" I turn around and look behind me. "How about going in the opposite direction? Will that take us to What's-his-name?"

"Yes, it will," Softy says, "after I arrange for your transportation. We do not have enough time to let you walk there and back."

"Transportation?" I say. "That sounds very interesting. Motorized, or horse-drawn?"

"On the wings of Gleamers," Softy says, with another chuckling quiver.

And I clutch for a moment. Another weirdness? Or finally some way out of it?

Chapter 6

WELL, SOFTY IS CERTAINLY right about how slow I am when I walk. And I'm at it again as we backtrack way down the road in reverse, heading once more for the outer edge of Gloomland.

I do my best, but it's still taking us quite a while to get there. And when I hear Softy mumbling to himself, I assume he's just trying to keep his complaining under wraps. But as we're finally nearing the edge, he tells me, "Just ahead, Les. Up there on the left, in that open field. They're waiting for us."

And I finally realize what he's been doing. Communicating with other Gleamers, for there they are, a group of eight, gathered around some kind of small, flat platform lying on the ground. But nothing with a motor on it, or two horses hitched up.

"I hesitate to ask," I say, "but what is that supposed to be?"

Another amused quiver twitters from Softy. "That is the platform you will lie upon. So try not to doze off, Les. And they are the engines you will need to fly there."

"Oh, wonderful!" I say. "No more weirdness!"

"That's right, Les," he says. "I'm glad you're pleased. Hurry and go join them. We do not have any time to waste."

But I still approach it rather slowly, trying to figure out what I am getting myself into, until one of the Gleamers calls to me. "Right this way! We're ready to go! Just lie down, and we'll do the rest."

Just lie down? But on what? It's not much bigger than a door, with what looks like a blanket thrown over it. Is that supposed to make it more comfortable? When I amble on over, trying to be casual, they all back away from it, apparently giving me space to lie down, as he had said I should. But lie down in what way? On my back? On my belly? Or upside-down?

I carefully bend over the platform, until I'm on my hands and knees, and I crawl a bit, until I get about to the middle, where I can lie down lengthwise, flat on my back, for Softy had said that I shouldn't doze off, and I almost always sleep on my belly. So here I am, all stretched out, on a platform that makes a rather hard bed, which has me hoping that the trip will not be a very long one.

I watch as the eight Gleamers divide into two groups, four along each side of the platform, where they somehow wiggle beneath it, until I can't see them anymore. But when the platform begins to rise off the ground, what clearly does come through to me is that the eight of them must be the engines that Softy said would be flying me there. And so I try to keep myself calm as the top of the platform starts slanting upwards, for they must be about to whisk me up and away on our flight to the mountain destination.

And then, without any warning, of course, the platform suddenly shoots up into the air, heading quickly toward the clouds overhead.

But without me on it. A great start.

When the platform had made its sudden move, I felt myself beginning to slip down it, heading toward its bottom edge, where I then slid off and fell thankfully onto the soft grass beneath it.

As I lie here, I can clearly see the eight of them underneath the platform, for they have halted the takeoff, and they are slowly bringing the platform back down.

When they land again, right next to me, all eight of them come spilling out, and I watch them circling around me, loudly quivering and twittering, as though they had just arrived at a great party in time for the opening joke.

One of them stops in front of me. "Sorry about that. This must be your first time."

"Yes," I say. "And probably my last."

"Like this one might have been," it says, with its hairs still quivering a bit, "if you had slipped off when we were about half way up to the clouds."

"Of course," I say. "How thoughtless of me. It could have been so much more amusing."

"All right," it says. "I understand. But we can't lose any more time, so let's give it another try. And this time, when you get onto the platform, instead of lying on your back, just turn over and reach up to get a firm grip on the top edge. Then all you will have to do is just hang on as tight as you possibly can."

Something, of course, that they should have told me before we took off. But I try to shake away the irritation I'm feeling, and I focus on getting back onto the platform, as he had directed.

No time to waste, indeed. And I'm pleased with how quickly I did get on, for before another moment could pass, I find myself hanging on for my life, as the platform, having slanted upward again, suddenly takes off, without a sound, except for the air that is streaming around me. The platform is shooting straight upward toward the clouds overhead, with a speed that leaves me gasping for breath. And a grip that is also being sorely tested, for I am not at all sure how long I can manage to hold on at this astonishing speed, not only up to the clouds we reach, but right on through them, into a clear and sun-filled sky above, where we finally level off, just in time for me to keep my grip in place.

I begin to look around for our destination, the mountain where Brian is supposed to be, and it's quite some time before I can spot the top of it peaking over the horizon. But if the platform keeps heading toward it at this still impressive pace, it should not be very long before we arrive.

And even less than that, for I'm beginning to see the entire mountain, a majestic one, glistening green, with trees and wide fields of grass, and with a peak that is capped, not with ice or snow, but with a small clearing right at the very top, one that could well be the landing spot where I will likely find Brian. He must be living up there in some kind of a shelter. Well, at least I assume so, as the platform heads right for that spot.

No radar, and no runway, and I can't see any landing lights, but apparently nothing is needed to help the platform land, for it swoops in down toward the clearing, a bit too fast for me, and then, turning sideways, it comes to a halt, just above the ground below it, where it slowly tips to the side and rolls me out onto a soft patch of grass.

Welcome to the mountain, I think, as I look around at the field I'm in. But with no sign of anyone else being here, I have to wonder if the platform has brought me to the wrong place. Not an unreasonable question to raise, considering all the crazy things that have led to my being here.

Well, I'm kind of stuck here now. So apparently it's up to me. And when only one thing comes to mind, I figure I might as well give it a try. Taking in a big breath, I holler out as loud as I can.

"Hey, Brian! Where are you!"

But I don't even get an echo back.

So what should I do now? Call out again? Or just keep sitting here, and hope that the other Gleamers have let him know I was coming? But when I remember how small they are, I begin to look more closely at the tree-line running around the outer edge of the clearing. And there he is, between two trees, on the upper part of the slope I am on.

The famous wise one, with two brains.

I wave and head his way, but as I approach him, he goes back into the trees, and then apparently waits for me there. It looks like he wants me to follow him, so I just trail after him as he takes me upward through the woods for quite a walk, almost to the very tip of the peak, where we come out of the woods again into another small clearing. And this one is quite different, for it has a small structure in it, his living quarters, I assume. And half of the structure is an open platform, with a rather large telescope on it, pointing up at the sky overhead.

Gesturing with a flick of his hairs to a chair standing next to the telescope, he tells me, "Sit."

As I go to the chair, I smile and nod my thanks, for the climb to get here has been a good workout for me, and sitting down is not only a nice relief. It also gives me a chance to take a closer look at Brian.

As I had been following him through the woods, I thought that it might have been a trick of the light, making him look quite different from the other Gleamers I've seen. But there is no question about it. All of Brian's hairs are gray, and he is somewhat smaller than the others. He looks more like a little old man to me. But a happy one, judging by his eyes, which return my look as I keep staring at him.

"Seen enough?" He sounds amused.

"Sorry," I say, "but you're quite a surprise."

"The hair," he says, "or the size of me?"

"How about both?" I say.

His hairs make a little chuckle. "Well, after more than a thousand years, we do tend to get a bit older."

I stare at him, my mouth half open.

"Only kidding," he says, with brightened eyes. "But enough of that. We need to get serious."

"Indeed we do," I say, "for the Gleamers are really in a tight spot, and they badly need your help."

"Your help, too, as I understand it," he says. "And that is why you have made the journey, so we can try to come up with something that will end this threat once and for all."

"Yes," I say. "And it looks like I've come to the right place." I point to the telescope. "Very impressive. It must give you a great view of the sky in the night."

"More than great," he says. "Absolutely fabulous. As an amateur astronomer, I love it up here. And not only to look at the stars, Les.

May I call you Les?"

"Of course," I say.

"I can also keep a good watch," he says, "on all the goings-on down below me."

"You mean," I say, "like what the Gleamers are up to? Can you really watch them from here, Brian?"

"And what the Glooms are also up to," he says.

"All right!" I say. "So does that mean I won't have

to fill you in? I mean, on what has brought me here?"

He looks at me a moment, and then he speaks very slowly, as though he is reciting a passage. "Whatever you can come up with, it will have to be something entirely new, not only to us, but also to them."

"Oh, no," I say. "Did you hear it from them? Or have you also started picking my brain?" I shake my head, but I have to smile.

"How about both?" he says. "Waste no words. Waste no time."

"Fair enough," I say. "So where do we start?"

"Perhaps," he says, "with the answer we need. The one you are still carrying around inside you."

Well, that certainly gets my attention. "Then pick away at my brain, please. I'd really like to see it, too."

He studies me as I sit there, leaning forward in my chair, until he finally nods once, and then breaks his silence. "Very interesting," he says. "Your mind, I mean. And how your emotions motivate it."

"If you say so." I have to smile again. "But apparently you have a better view. I'm generally left outside of it, and it rarely invites me in anymore."

"Because you no longer value who is in it?" He pauses, as though he's looking closer. "All those enlightening conversations, the ones you have had with such wonderful people. It's all still there, Les, inside of you, with the light that you had so openly treasured, before you closed the lid on the chest, where you are now keeping them."

"The ones, you mean, that led me down this dead

43

end road I'm on?" I'm frowning, caught up in the same old argument I have had too often with
myself.

"Another important problem," he says, "involving the pathway that you are on. But what about your three letters?"

"What do you mean?" I say. "My applications? The ones I sent out looking for a job?" I wave my hand, like I'm brushing away a fly. "I didn't get a single reply. Not even one answer."

"You're right, Les," he says. "You did not get one. But how about two, then?"

I shake my head. It's getting to me. "If I'm going to dream, then how about ten?"

"Whatever the number," he says, "we must put it aside for now. We need to get back to the answer you do have."

"I still don't understand," I say. "What answer do you think I have?"

"Something," he says, "that must be entirely new to them."

"But that still leaves me in the dark," I say. "I simply have no way of knowing. So maybe I should just walk around and find one of them that I could ask."

His eyes appear to open wider, like I have somehow surprised him. "But you have already done that, Les."

"No," I say. "Not him. He didn't tell me anything. He didn't even say a word. And I could hardly see him where he was sitting, down there in the dark."

"Keep going, Les," he says. "You are almost there.

Tell me what you did next."

"Oh," I say. "You mean my lighter? But I just flicked it on so I could see his face better."

"And what did he do then?" One of his front hairs comes up, and he wiggles it at me.

"Of course," I say. "I see what you're after. He reached out to touch the flame, like he had never seen it before. Something entirely new to him? But it was such a tiny flame. I just don't get your point at all."

"Time to end our conversation," he says. "I need to send you back down. So let us make our way to the platform."

"Without any answer?" I'm getting upset.

"Oh," he says, "I'll give you something to think about as you make your trip. And by the time you land, Les, I believe you will have turned it into what you are seeking."

Still troubled, and filled with doubt, I follow him down to the platform, and once again I get myself settled onto it, with another firm grip on the top.

"It has been a pleasure," he says, "to chat with you."

But I cannot come up with any response as I lay there with a sense of failure stifling my thoughts.

When the platform rises a bit, letting me know that the engines are once again in place, Brian moves closer to the side of it, near to where I have my head. "Yes," he says. "I have not forgotten. And it comes from one of your favorite people, someone you met very early in your life. So listen to what he taught you then."

I grip the top of the platform even harder, as I wait to hear who it is.

In a sing-song voice, Brian tells me, "Jack be nimble. Jack be quick. So make them jump over candlesticks."

And the platform suddenly tilts up, taking me once more toward the clouds.

Chapter 7

SOMETHING, INDEED, TO THINK about. Brian's final comments to me. Wise words from the double
brain. But I'm wondering if maybe he might have
used only one of them for some answer I left behind
when I departed.

All the way down on my return journey, until the
platform finally lands and comes to a full stop on the
grass, I have been trying to push away the feeling of
how empty it has left me. But then, of course, as I
should have expected, it just gets much worse, when
I see Softy rushing out to the platform to greet me
with joyful eyes, and how quickly he comes to a halt,
when he sees the look on my face.

As I had told Brian, my mind rarely invites me in
these days, but it must be Softy's deep disappointment that opens the door, and I can see what is going on in there. The Gloom, sitting in the dark. My
lighter held up to his face. His hand reaching out to
touch… Wait a minute. Was that it? Yes, of course.

The missing part. Brian was spelling it out for me. Jack be nimble, Jack be quick, for there's a flame on each candlestick.

It brings forth a big smile from me, which also brings Softy nearer. He comes right next to the platform, where I'm sitting up on the edge of it. When I see that his eyes are once again filled with hope, I recall something else that I think will cheer him up even more. It's from a book I had read way back in my teens, not an assigned one in my class, but a title on one of the library shelves that had caught my eye.

"Softy," I say, "what just came to mind is a book I once read a long time ago. And it had the title *The Art of War*."

"Good!" Softy says. "That sounds just right. And it tells me that you haven't given up, as I thought you had when I first saw you."

I smile again, to show him he is right. "It was written by a man named Sun Tzu, who said that all warfare is based on deception. And he offered, among many other things, this particular bit of advice on how to win a conflict:

Hold out baits to entice the enemy.
Feign disorder, and then crush him.

And that," I say, "is exactly what I think we should do with the Glooms."

Softy's hairs are all quivering wildly. "And how will we do it, Les? How will we crush them?"

"It will take a great deal of work," I say, "but we're going to make it happen." And I carefully explain to him, step by step, the strategy I have in mind for luring the Gloomers into the trap we will set. I also share with him my main concern. Do we have enough time?

"Just turn us loose," he says, "and we'll show you how fast we really are." He's beaming at me, and he's leaning toward me, like he's about to run the hundred yard dash.

"Then let's return to your territory, as quickly as we can," I say, "for we will need to get the others involved." And for the first time now, whatever the odds, I believe that what we're about to bring off is no longer just a dream.

Since Softy lets them know we will soon be arriving, all the Gleamers are already there, keeping a multitude of eyes on the pathway that comes out of the woods and then slopes on down for quite a distance into the center of Gleamer territory, where they have now gathered. When we come into view, the first ones to spot us start waving their hairs and twittering together, giving us a warm welcome as we start heading down toward them. They are all together in the middle of their territory, a wide, level field of soft grass, surrounded by pleasant woods, with the usual spread of scraggly bushes growing along the outer edge of the clearing. As we pass the edge, I stop for a moment, and I snap off a couple of small twigs that I put into my pocket.

Going on into the field, I'm pleased to see only one other pathway leading back into the woods at the far end.

"Looks good for our strategy," I say to Softy. "It gives us control over where they will enter." I have to smile to myself, sounding like some kind of military planner.

"You must be a graduate of West Point," Softy says, looking away as he quivers a smile.

"Yes," I say, "and reporting for duty to my superior officer." When I salute him, he turns away, like he's brushing it off, but I can see how much it pleased him.

As I approach the group, they all turn toward me, without making another sound. All of their eyes are on me, as they wait to hear what I will say. It's such a new experience for me, such an intensely felt one, that it leaves me even more deeply aware of how crucial this moment is for them.

I raise my hand and give them all a friendly wave, and they each return it with a few lifted hairs. "I hope I am speaking loudly enough, for I want every one of you to hear me. And that is exactly what it will take, every one of you, to complete what we must put together to stop the Glooms now, once and for all."

Apparently, they can't hold back. They all have to twitter away, letting me know what it means to them. The end of their seemingly endless threat.

I wave again to quiet them down. "But time is running out for us. So let me tell you what needs to be done, beginning with step one. I can start a small fire for a few of you. That will be the easy part. But then, at a moment's notice, those few must be able, with the help of others, to spread it around to everyone else. And, by that point, you must all have learned how to keep each of your fires going."

No response at all, of course. Just the puzzled look in their eyes.

"But what, you may wonder, is a fire, and how are we going to use it against them." I do get a response now. A lot of nodding, and glancing at each other.

"Well," I say, "to save some time, I'll have Softy explain it all to you, since he can communicate directly with you. And while he's doing that, I would like to walk in among you, right to the very middle of you, and then have you all form a big circle around me. Can you do that for me now, please?"

They are more than cooperative, and very swift, too, for by the time I have reached the middle, they have closed me into a well-formed circle, where I stand, waiting until Softy has finished filling them in. Then I dig down into my pocket to bring out the couple of twigs I had put there, and I hold them up high for all of them to see.

"This," and I have to raise my voice, "is step two, for you must gather these small twigs, mixed in with small branches, from all the scraggly plants around us, and on into the woods. And after you have helped to lay a carpet of them down onto this entire area within your circle, each of you must then build your own pile of them, a rather large pile, right in front of where you are standing. And there must be no gaps at all between your piles."

I pause a moment, groping. Am I making it clear

enough to them, what it is that we should be aiming for? Not at all sure, I give it another try.

"What we absolutely need, before the Glooms arrive here, is an unbroken ring of twigs and branches running around in front of you, with a carpeting of twigs also covering the circled ground. If you can bring that off by the time they get here, you will not only have completely surrounded them with wood. You will also have built a coffin for them."

I hear a loud and happy quivering running back and forth among them. So maybe I'm getting through, with only one final point to stress.

"But here is the toughest part of the challenge." That stops all the quivering. "With very little time to achieve it, the top of the ring must be at least twice as tall as the biggest members among you."

Glancing down at myself, I can see exactly what that means. To achieve the goal I have set for them, they will have to build the entire circle of twigs and branches at least as high as my waist. Was that possible? And could they find enough twigs?

"Les!" I hear, and I look around. Softy is coming quickly toward me.

"What, Softy?" He looks so troubled. "What's happened? Is it—"

"Yes, Les!" And his eyes tell me. "They're coming, a column of them. Two by two, and they have it with them. The mobile one!"

"All right," I say, "so they're coming," as I look out at the others again. "But that doesn't mean we're lost yet. Just remember how slow they are, and you can still bring it off. Each and every one of you, laying the carpet, and building up your own pile. Just give it your very best, and—" Before I can finish, they're darting out in all directions away from the center, filling the air with the sound of a buzz-saw that has grown a pair of wings.

Chapter 8

AS I STAND HERE, I watch the impossible happening. The ground within their circle is suddenly covered with a thin layer of twigs and branches, and I can actually see it rising, slowly but steadily. My turn, then, to hurry over before the twigs are all gone, and, after breaking off two good handfuls, I take them back to a place just outside the circle, where I put them into a small pile on the ground, directly across from where I hope the Glooms will be entering. Then I dig a bit deeper into my left pocket, and I take out the mighty weapon they have never seen before. Standing there, I hold it up, as I wait for the right moment. A powerful army of large Glooms is marching this way now, and what will bring them all to their knees? My little lighter, with its tiny flame.

Or am I just kidding myself?

After each of their piles finally reaches the height we want, the sloping path we came down earlier is blocked by the completed circle. And so, to make a new entryway there, the piles at that spot are shifted outward a bit, like two welcoming doors swung open that can also be quickly pushed closed, after the Glooms have all entered.

But what strikes me is a troubling thought. What if they don't come down the road? What if they choose to go into the woods, on either side of the road, and make their way down through the trees, trying to catch us off balance? I'm gripped by the thought, until I remember what Softy said, that they were coming with the Light Destructor. So wouldn't that likely keep them out of the woods, and on the road?

They answer the question for me, as they come into view at the top of the slope, behind something slowly moving along in front of them. From where I'm standing, still at a distance, it looks like some kind of a sled, a large one, with a long rectangular box on it, almost as big as it is. On each side of the sled, a Gloom is walking close to it, apparently trying to keep it on the road, with two more of them pushing it from the rear. And just behind the four of them, from what I can see, a growing crowd of other Glooms appears to be gathering quickly up there, as though they don't want to miss out on any of the fun that is about to begin. And when the size of the crowd just keeps growing, I have to wonder if Gloomland is emptying out every last one of them, sending them off to the top of our road, where they are about to descend upon us, as we had feared.

As one of the Glooms up there takes the first step

onto the sloping road, coming into full view, I find it hard once again to believe what I'm seeing. I had laughed at Softy's description, but the Gloom up there did look like an unwrapped mummy, one who has just walked out of a tomb, bringing the darkness of the tomb with him, for a shadow is dimming the daylight around him.

"Softy!" I cry out. "It's fire time! Let's get them all going now!" Bending over my small pile of twigs, I click on my lighter, holding it steady, until the twigs begin to catch fire, letting me back away in time for two Gleamers carrying twigs to put the ends of theirs into the fire.

"Remember," I say, "you have to move slowly. If you try to hurry, the flames will go out."

As these two move carefully away, two more arrive with their twigs, and I stand here watching how quickly they learn, for I am soon no longer the only place where a burning pile can be found. Around the entire circle, Gleamers are carrying away flames from many other piles and taking them back to their own. And I can see how effectively they are doing it, until all of them have finally stopped, and they're waiting to hear what they should do next, for every pile of their twigs is beginning to burn. Softy then has half of them, those who can be seen from the road, go back around the circle to stay out of sight.

A well-timed move, indeed, for the Glooms are pushing the sled down the sloping road, with all the others falling in behind them. And they don't let up as they make their descent, awkwardly bumping into each other, wobbling and dragging their feet along, all the way down the road, until they are finally approaching the open doorway through the twigs. And that stops them right there, as they keep looking into the circle, apparently trying to spot what they have come to destroy, a gathering of all the Gleamers, with their lights on. I think they might also be a bit leery about all of those lights being focused on them.

Directly across from the doorway, Softy has three of the Gleamers push their small piles of burning twigs under the large piles in front of them, starting a bigger fire.

When the Glooms see the light from it beginning to brighten, it must look to them like they have found their target. Wanting to destroy it before it gets too bright, they push the sled quickly into the middle of the circle, and then they wait there, while the two Glooms hurry to remove the front end of the box being carried on it. The other Glooms, who have also been crowding in through the entryway, are spreading out on both sides, apparently anxious to watch what their new device will do to that irritating light.

Softy gives the signal, and the Gleamers who had been keeping out of sight stream back around to the front, where they quickly close the entryway by pushing the opened doors of piled twigs back into place.

A crucial moment, for the Glooms could easily smash through any entryway they choose to make, and the only way to stop them from breaking out is to startle them with something they have never seen or felt before. A very large and extremely hot fire.

Softy signals once again, and, with their always swift response, all of the Gleamers start pushing their small piles of burning twigs into and under their large piles. With so much more above them, the flames quickly spread up through each pile, and also onto the carpeting of twigs covering the entire area. The inferno being created around them clearly has all of the Glooms confused, not only by the strange light, but also by the feeling of the intense heat. It is something they have never encountered before, and it is growing stronger and coming closer with every passing moment.

As they frantically try, in all directions, to move back away from it, this new and deadly combination reaches an intensity so extreme that something completely unexpected suddenly begins to happen.

Some Glooms who are much too close to me, just a few steps inside the burning circle, are undergoing a remarkable change. I had expected to see the threat in their eyes glistening out at me again, but the fire has apparently turned their eyes completely dark. And for another big surprise, perhaps the biggest one of all, I can see that the Glooms are beginning to cry. But they are not crying tears. They are crying drops of darkness.

Softy had told me that when he had tried to look into a Gloomer's mind, there was nothing in there he could see, except the darkness filling his mind.

But that darkness clearly has to be something much more than just an absence of light, something perhaps with a force of its own, as it keeps spilling out of their eyes. Like a pot boiling over from too much heat, it starts flowing steadily down their faces and onto their bodies. And then it begins to spread out there, like a magician's cape, until one by one they start disappearing behind it.

Glancing around at the others, who have been tearfully spreading their own darkness throughout the circle, I watch them, until they are all finally hidden from sight.

"Amazing!" Softy says. He is there beside me again.

I can't see into the darkness any more, but I can still hear something that comes from there, and it stops my breath. It's the sound of things dropping onto the carpet of flickering flames.

As I stand there quietly next to Softy, I realize that I'm still holding my breath.

"Did you hear it?" Softy whispers to me.

"Yes," I say, easing out the word.

"But was it just one of them? What about the others?" He's staring at me, pleading with me, wanting to hear me say it. Yes, Softy, all of them. It's finally and absolutely true.

But when I look into the circle again, all I can see is the darkness that is still keeping the light away. How then, I wonder, can we be sure?

"Tell me something, Softy," I say. "How long will it take for that darkness in the circle to disappear?"

The question makes him twitch a bit, for he knows why I am asking it. He looks up and studies the sky. "That whole bank of puffy clouds is going to take its time, Les. But not much more than half an hour, before the sun shines forth again. And then it will be just a matter of minutes. About as long it took to get the darkness out of your hand. That is, if you still remember it."

I try to hold in my smile, as I offer him a deep frown. "Of course, you can't be serious," I say. "You know how remarkable my memory is." And it's my turn to look up at the sky. "But what did I just ask you, Softy? Something about a cloud, I think."

"Yes," Softy says, "the one in your head."

"Of course," I say. "That special cloud. The only one with a silver lining."

"Now you're talking!" Softy says. "Just blow that one out of your left ear, and we'll have ourselves a real winner!"

We both share a chuckle, enjoying the bantering, and it helps us keep our anxious thoughts away from having to wait out the time.

‑◦❧❦◦‑

Chapter 9

Softy, of course, is right on the mark, for as we approach the half hour, the bank of clouds has just about passed, and the sun is breaking into the open, sending its rays down into the darkness still filling the circle.

I'm getting quite excited, as I see the darkness thinning out. But I'm also feeling a bit concerned. I mean, what if some of the Glooms in there are still alive? They won't be very happy when they see the two of us standing here, staring at them.

"Softy," I say, "keep an eye open. I'm going to grab some more of the twigs and get another fire going. If any of them is still moving in there, we may have to defend ourselves." And I head back toward the hedges encircling the area.

But even before I get there, I can already see the problem. All the hedges have been stripped rather clean. "It's going to take me some time, Softy."

"No need to hurry," he says.

And that stops me. Is it all over? That would be

very good news, indeed. But not, I imagine, a very pretty scene. "How bad does it look, Softy?"

"Absolutely terrible," he says.

"Must be a pretty gory sight." I try not to picture it.

"No," he says. "Not gory at all."

"What do you mean?" I'm starting back now.

"Take a look for yourself," he says.

And when I do, it really stuns me.

The circle is empty. The Glooms are all gone. All that is left is their big device, tipped over onto one of its sides, and with smoke still coming out of it. It had to be the thud we heard.

"Softy!" I almost yell it. "What's going on here? They may be weird, but they can't just disappear."

"All right, Sherlock," Softy says. "Since you know how he solved every one of his cases, it's your turn now to give it a try."

"Not a good time for bantering," I say, too upset, and getting irritated. But then I see the hurt in Softy's eyes, and I try to calm down. "Sorry about that, Doctor Watson. I just didn't know what I should do next. If I only had my deerstalker hat, and my pipe to puff on thoughtfully, I could solve this case before you could blink."

"But that would give you forever," he says, "for I never blink. I don't know how. Another case for you to solve?"

"Maybe after we figure out this one." I look around the circle. "What would Sherlock have done next?"

"A clue!" Softy says, with one hair raised, like a

single finger stressing the point. "What you need to do first is to find a clue."

"But not just any clue," I say. "A special one, like he always finds, that leads him right to the final solution."

With that in mind, I step over the ring of ashes left from the large piles of twigs that had circled the area. And I slowly walk around it, carefully looking for that giveaway clue, until I come back to where I had started, with nothing new that I could find. The ring of ashes had not been disturbed in any way that I could see. The only break in the ring was still the entryway that had been opened to let the Glooms into the circle. But there was no indication at all of anything else having been disturbed. It was all exactly as we had left it, the circle complete, the entryway opened, the—wait a minute! And it finally hits me.

"Softy!" I say. "It's the entryway! Thank you, Sherlock!"

I run a bit too quickly across the circle to the entryway, and as I stop for a moment to huff and puff, I glance down to find Softy already beside me, anxiously waiting for me to keep going.

"Don't you ever rest?" I say, still trying to catch my breath. "What's your secret? Tell me, Softy." I want to keep him talking. For just a few more moments more.

"It's alright," he says. "You can stall , if you want. It's what I like about you, Les. You're not very good at fooling me."

I have to smile at that one. "Okay, a big point for you. But let's get back to the clue now. We need to see where it will lead us."

"Where what will lead us?" Softy says. "You haven't told me what it is yet."

"The ashes, Softy." And I feel the excitement returning again. "We had the Glooms all caught in the circle, with the flames around them taking a terrible toll. When the darkness within them came out to form that cloud hanging over the circle, we saw every one of them disappear into it. And that was where we expected to find them, when the sun finally came out."

"An excellent summary," Softy said, "from an obviously superior mind. But why do you stop there? We need to know what happened to them."

"And that," I say, "brings us back to the ashes, for while the piles of twigs were still burning down, dropping their ashes onto the ground in an unbroken circle around the Glooms, someone opened the entryway again to let all the Glooms back out before the flames completely destroyed them. And when the Glooms walked out through that entryway—"

"Yes!" he says, his hairs bristling, as he feels his own excitement rising. "You got it, Les. Nice going." And he's smiling, as he waits for me to fill him in further.

But, before I do, I hold back a moment, wanting to bring him into it more. "What do I have? I don't quite get it yet."

"The answer," he says, "to your clue, Les."

"And what is that?" I'm frowning.

"What happened when the Glooms walked out. They all had to trample across those ashes. And when they did, they must have left a trail. At least a faint one. Yes, of course." He's looking at me more closely. "Or are you pulling my leg again? You know I don't have a leg to pull. So what's going on here, Les?"

"I wouldn't pull your leg," I say, "even if you had one. What's going on here, I hope, should be a lot more interesting to both of us. And certainly a lot more challenging."

My turn to study him, as we both try to look more deeply into each other's eyes. And what I see there, as I expected, strongly encourages me to keep going.

"Softy," I say, "how would you like to go hunting for some half-cooked Glooms?"

"I thought you'd never ask, Les." He slowly moves closer to the entryway, with me right behind him.

And there it is, the faint trail that they had made when they left.

I glance at Softy, and he nods to me. Both of us can see it, heading off a short way to the right, and then on into the woods over there. As I had hoped, we should be able to follow it. But not very far, I guess, since the Glooms will keep stomping the ashes away.

With Softy beside me, I step over the ashes still there, and we follow the trail to the edge of the woods, as I feel my excitement peaking again. They obviously have had a big head-start, and that makes me walk as fast as I can. With my eyes locked onto the trail, and with Softy easily keeping up with me, it looks like we'll be able to catch up with them. But what will we do, if we can?

We keep moving right along, but the trail is getting more difficult to follow, and when we come to a clearing in the woods, a small field of grass among the trees, it looks as though we will lose it there. Making our way into the field, until we're almost halfway across it, we can find no further signs of the ashes among the grass.

But as we look up, we both feel a shiver, like a winter wind has just hit us hard, for what we can see, as I had hoped, is something a lot more interesting. And certainly a lot more challenging.

The Glooms we have been trying to track are coming out of the woods in a single file, with each of them reaching back to hold the hand of the Gloom right behind him, forming a long chain of them that the first Gloom is now leading around the outer edge of the field we are in. He continues circling the area until he finally closes the loop by reaching out and taking the hand of the last Gloom in the chain, leaving Softy and me completely surrounded.

Apparently, we are the ones who were being tracked, and we have stumbled right into the middle of it.

As I'm looking around for another way that might let us get out of there, Softy nudges lightly against me. "Not a chance, Les. They have us trapped. But since I'm the one who got you into this mess, it's up to me to help you get out." Raising up one of his hairs, he points to where we had entered the field. "You see those two Glooms by the trail? I'm going to crash into them, and try to make an opening for you. If you can just get yourself back onto the trail, you'll be faster than any one of them."

I reach down and put my hand on him. "Not yet, Softy. There's something wrong here. Something different. You better wait."

"What, Les?" he says. "I don't see it."

"That's it!" I say. "Neither do I. Just look at their eyes. Right into them. What you always tell me not to do."

Softy turns to check it out. "Les, you're right! The threat, I mean. What's happened to it? I can't see it."

When I look again, only one thing has changed. The head Gloom has stepped out of the chain, and he's heading directly toward us.

"Careful," Softy says. "Maybe he can still turn it on."

But as the Gloom gets near, he surprises us both, for he holds up

his hands, like he wants to surrender. And at that moment, I see who it is. The Gloom with only one eye. "Softy, I know this one. He's the Gloom I clicked my lighter on in front of his face."

"Yes," Softy says. "But what's he up to?"

The Gloom stops in front of me, making me want to back away, but all he does is lean forward and look closely into my eyes. Then he holds up his right hand before me, and he points with his other hand to a fingertip on it. As he makes a low grunting sound, he jerks his hand quickly away, and then he nods to me.

I glance down at Softy. "What's that supposed to mean?"

"Les," he says, clearly excited again. "He's checking you out. He wants to be sure. Were you the one who showed him the lighter? I can hardly believe it. Do you know what that means? The two of you are communicating!"

I look again at the Gloom, and he nods once more. "That's it, Softy! Most likely a first! He's opening a dialogue with me."

"Very, very interesting," Softy says. "So keep it going, Les. What does he want?"

"And what do we want?" I say. "I mean, they're still all here. But where has the threat gone? What about that?"

"Give it a try, Les," Softy says. "You might get an answer from him."

"Okay," I say. "Why not?" I raise my finger, showing it to the Gloom, and I slowly point around at all the Glooms in the chain. When he looks at them, and then back at me, I open my eyes as widely as I can, and I cringe in fear at the sight of the Glooms.

He stands there, watching me for a moment, as though he's trying to figure it out. And when he shakes his head, I think I've lost him. But he's pointing to his own eye, and then once again around the circle, apparently to all of their eyes, and when he looks back at me, he squints until his one eye is almost completely closed.

It's my turn to figure it out. "What are you trying to tell me?" I say. "That all the Glooms are blind?" And I cover both of my eyes with my hands.

But he shakes his head again, and he squints once more to show me that his eye is still open a little. So I cover my eyes again with my hands, but I crack open a small space between two of my fingers, and when I look at him through the crack, he nods again. Then he holds up the tip of his finger that had touched the flame, and he points once more to all the Glooms in the chain, before jerking his fingertip back again.

Like the last piece of a jigsaw puzzle, it all finally fits together for me, as I keep nodding, with a smile, to show him it has.

But not yet for Softy, who has been watching it all. "Only got some of it, Les," he tells me. "How about you? Did you get the rest?"

"I think so," I say. "But not all of it. For what's happened is almost unbelievable. We thought all the Glooms had been destroyed by the flames, something they had never seen before. But my one-eyed friend here had already seen fire, in the small flame from my lighter, and he also knew how much it hurt him. So when he saw the little piles already burning in front of each Gleamer, it must have kept him outside of the ring, when all the others went in. And when he could see, even with his only eye, how the bigger fires had trapped them in there, he must have been the one who opened the entryway again, and got every one of them back out. But not before it had badly damaged all of their threatening eyes. End of story? I don't think so. For Softy, it's changed your entire world."

"For the good?" he says. "Or the bad, Les? I think I'll

hold off on that part. At least until I can see for myself."

"And that," I say, "should not take long, for I think it will likely depend on what happens next." I turn back to my one-eyed friend again, and after a backward wave of my hand around at all the other Glooms, I point first to where he had earlier come out of the woods at the head of the chain, and then to the trail that had brought us there. When he looks at both of them, and then back at me, I have each of my pointing fingers raised, and I'm waiting now to see if he understands what I am asking him. Where are you going with them? Which direction will you be taking? I can't think of any other way to ask him.

He shakes his head and turns away, as though he's going to leave me hanging there. But then he raises his arm, and he points off now in a new direction through the woods.

I look down at Softy. "Any idea? I mean, if he leads them into the woods there, where do you think he'll be taking them?"

"No doubt about it," Softy says. "If he takes them off in that direction, and he goes for not too long a way, they're going to be walking right back into Gloomland."

"Of course," I say. "Where else could he take them? The fire, he said, left them almost blind. And that will forever doom them now to stay in their own familiar place, where they can at least still find their way around."

"World-changing, indeed," Softy says.

I turn to the Gloom, smiling now, and I hold out my hand to him, wanting to show him how pleased I am with what he is doing

He takes my hand, and, as he stands there holding it, he raises his other hand and touches me on the cheek.

Softy has been taking it all in. "No kissing allowed, Les."

When I nod to the Gloom, a slow one to end the moment, he turns around and makes his way across the field, taking his place again at the head of the chain. As we watch him now, he leads all the Glooms once more around the edge of the clearing, and then into the woods at the place he had pointed out to us. We stand there, until we can see the end of the chain enter the woods. And when it does, we know that he has them all heading back to Gloomland now.

"Les," Softy says, "I must be dreaming."

—◦ ❧ ◦—

Chapter 10

SOFTY AND I HAVE returned back to his own territory, and we are making our way down the sloping road to where the Gleamers have all gathered in the field at the bottom of it. They have come to hear the special report he has told them I will be making, and that is what has caused the little argument we are having.

"No, Softy," I tell him, trying to sound firm. "It just wouldn't be right."

"Right or wrong," he says. "That isn't the issue. It's who most deserves to tell them about it."

"Exactly," I say. "And that means you."

"Les," he says, "I must insist on this, or I won't be able to feel good about it. So help me out here. Make the report."

"Well," I say, "you certainly know how to twist an arm, even though you don't have one."

"No arm," he says. "That's true. But a clever mind. It makes all the difference."

"Sure," I say, "You're a fast learner. Just look at how

much I have taught you, Softy."

"No need," he says. "I've made a list. And I keep it tucked under one of my hairs. Including every spot you stumbled into, where I had to get you out of it."

"Stumbled blindly into, you mean?" I say. "I'm pleased to hear you admit it, Softy, that you recognize how well I had set up that trap for them."

"Exactly right back at you," he says. "Nobody else can explain it better. So that's why I'm putting you on the spot now. And don't try to fake your way out of it."

Before I can stop him, Softy moves quickly right to the edge of the field before us, and he raises his voice now, with a big shimmering of his hairs. "How pleased I am to see you all here, and to introduce our very special guest."

A soft rippling of hairs from the audience.

"He has come to us," Softy says, "from another world, one that we desperately appealed to for help when the Glooms were going to move against us. And we could not have made a better choice, as he will now explain to you."

When Softy moves back, I have no choice. Stepping forward, I give them all a big smile and a friendly wave, and I hear another soft rippling from them. I remind myself to speak out to the furthest Gleamer away from me, so they can all hear what I'm going to say. "I must begin by first telling you something that I ask you all to keep firmly in mind. The report I am about to give you will be coming from both Softy and me, for we each played a part in what has happened."

I glance around, but I can't see any more movement among them, not even the flick of a single hair. It's as though they are all holding their breath, hoping to hear something really special. So I give it to them, short and sweet. "Your entire world has been changed, for the Glooms are no longer a threat to you."

I expected a major roar from them, with a lot of swirling and spinning around, as they finally could let their feelings out, having held them in for so terribly long. But what I see surprises me, for they all seem to be frozen into place.

I turn to Softy, with a questioning look.

"Keep talking," he says. "They just can't believe it. You better tell them how it happened."

"All right," I say, turning back to them, and speaking out again. "When you heard that the Glooms were not destroyed in the fire, you must have thought they had all escaped. But the truth is that the fire had already badly damaged their eyes, almost completely blinding them, so I tell you now once again. They are no longer a threat to you. And you also have a new friend who is their leader, a one-eyed Gloom who never entered the fire. He very much wants the Glooms and the Gleamers to live in peace with each other, and to show you he means it, he has already taken them all back to Gloomland, which they will never be able to leave again."

Well, that did it. The major roar. Their hairs are flapping so wildly now that I think they're all about to take off. And when they finally quiet down enough,

I raise my hand, and I speak up again.

"I hope, indeed, that their new leader will be at least half as good as yours. Since the moment I first arrived here, your leader has shown me, time and again, how effective he is at keeping you all so well informed about everything. And I have also just learned how brave he is. When the Glooms had both of us surrounded, and it looked like the end for us, he told me to get ready, for he was going to smash himself into two of them so that I could get away free. How very lucky you all are to have such a wonderful leader."

Someone in the group, off to the left, calls out his name. "Softy!" And others scattered around the gathering start joining in until they are all loudly chanting it together.

"Softy! Softy! Softy!"

Turning, I gesture to him. "Come on, Softy. Say a few words."

He comes forward, very slowly, but his eyes, filled with happiness, are clearly beaming at me.

When I start to back away, he says, "Please, Les, stay with me. Or I will have to leave."

I stop then. "All right, Softy. It's your day."

"No, Les, it's our day." He looks out at the gathering that has quieted down and is waiting to hear what he will say. "I have asked Les to stay beside me, for the two of us have become like one. And he can help me with whatever questions you might like to ask me, until it is time for him to go home."

"Where is that?" someone asks.

Softy turns and gestures to me. "You're on, Les. It's answer time."

I nod, and I turn back to the group. "Home is my other world," I say, "where I came from to visit you here, when I got your message asking for help."

That brings forth another question. "Which world is your real one?"

"Apparently," I say, "like Softy and me, the two of them are somehow one, each of them needing the other to complete the real world."

Another voice. "And when will you return to yours?"

I look at Softy. "You're on now."

"Soon," he says, looking back at me. And the happiness is gone from his eyes.

"Oh, my very good friend," I say. "I may be going back to my world, but you'll always be just a dream away."

"Which brings us," he says, "to your afternoon nap."

"But I'm not at all tired," I say.

"A nice soft patch of grass here," he says, "may well change your mind."

"A nice Softy patch of grass?" I say. "Okay, let's give it a try."

"And don't forget," he says, "to check your mail there."

"My mail?" I'm frowning at him.

"You'll see," he says, "what Brian told you. Not even one. But how about two?"

Confused, as usual, I shake my head, and I lower myself onto what is, indeed, a very soft patch. As I remember how I first got here, something once again is closing my eyes, shutting out everything around me, including my last glance at Softy. But is it going to take me back to my world? Or just drop me into another dream?

Fortunately, it keeps me waiting again for only a few moments, until I can open my eyes once more and look around. But there is no sigh of relief this time, for here I am, once again, back in my room above the garage, stretched out onto my lumpy bed, and staring up at a terribly uninteresting ceiling.

So will that be it? I can't help wondering. Another big disappointment for me? Why couldn't it have changed my world, at least some small part of it? Maybe not as much as the Gleamer's world. But more than just letting me wake up with the thought that it was only a dream. A new one, yes. But what does that mean, if it's tucked away, like all the others, in the darkness back there in my mind?

I can feel my thoughts moving around back there, like the Glooms have found a way into my room, and I close my eyes again, wanting to escape them. But then a bright light suddenly comes on in the room, and when I open my eyes to see what it is, I almost let out a loud cheer, for everything around me is glowing once more.

It has to be Softy. But what does it mean? The glow is not blinking any kind of message, like the way he had sent me the SOS. It's just a steady and very welcome one. And I think that's what he's telling me.

He's still with me. I haven't lost him.

Remembering his last words, I get out of bed to check my mail.

Downstairs, beside the doorway up to my room, I have a small box, fastened to the wall, that the mailman uses for my mail. When I get there and I lift the lid, I reach inside without looking, for I don't expect to find anything in there. But what I take out are the envelopes from two of the publishers. And I carry them back up to my room, trying not to make too much of it. Well, I think, at least they did respond. But after a few skipped heartbeats, I hastily tear them open to find that both of them are inviting me to come in for an interview. And the position they each have open? An editor in their publishing house. My dream come true.

But wait just a minute here. What am I saying? It's not just another dream for me. It's what I had deeply hoped for, when I returned from what I thought was only a dream about a different world. After living in the old, and having visited the new, I have finally awakened within the real world, a merging of my old existence with every one of my new hair-raising friends, who have changed my life so completely. Including, of course, the most special one of all, who will be waiting to hear the good news I have.

Thank you, Softy, for being there, as I will always be here for you.

An old world and a new world. We have glued them both together with love.

What a good way to end the day.

About the Author

William Glasser received his PhD in English, with a minor in Comparative Religions, through the Writer's Workshop at the University of Iowa, his MA in Creative Writing at the University of Florida, and his BA at Harpur College, part of the SUNY system. Dr. Glasser taught for many years at Williams College, Skidmore College, and Trinity College in Hartford. He was also awarded a Senior Fulbright Lectureship and taught American literature to Austrian students for a year at the University of Salzburg, Austria. Currently, he is President Emeritus of Southern Vermont College. In addition to two books of literary criticism, he has published critical articles, short stories, and poetry in a variety of scholarly and popular journals in the United States, Austria, and South Korea. His last academic book, The Art of Literary Thieving, can be found in the libraries of Harvard, Yale, Princeton, and fifty other U.S. universities, including many other institutions in Canada, in European countries, and in the Far East (thank you Google).

www.ingramcontent.com/pod-product-compliance
Lightning Source LLC
Chambersburg PA
CBHW031241260626
47169CB00007B/2400